Mari's Big Idea

A Journey from Fear to Courage

Author: Mariana McWilliams

To all the young dreamers, doers, and big thinkers out there—

This book is for you! Remember, every idea starts small, just like a tiny seed. With courage, kindness, and a sprinkle of imagination, you can turn your ideas into something amazing.

Keep dreaming, keep growing, and always believe in yourself. You have the power to make a difference and brighten the world in your own special way.

With love and encouragement,
From Mari's Gold

Mari, an intelligent and ambitious 12-year-old, had big dreams but was afraid of accomplishing them. One day, while journaling, she heard the familiar melody of an ice cream truck. Mari thought to herself, "I want something sweet, but just not ice cream". Suddenly, a light bulb went off in her head, "SNOW CONES! Who wouldn't want a frozen treat in the hot Phoenix, Arizona heat?" Mari thought to herself.

Every time Mari thought about running her own snow cone stand, her stomach filled with butterflies." I don't even have any supplies. What if I make a mistake?" "What if I say too much? What if I don't say enough? What if I fail!"

Later that day, as Mari and her dad sat on a park bench, watching the sun set, she confessed her fears about running her own snow cone stand. Mari sighed. "What if I make a mistake? What if I say too much? What if I don't say enough? What if I fail?"

Her dad smiled. "Do you remember when you first started playing the flute and couldn't get a sound out?" Mari nodded. "But now, you play beautifully. Sometimes, you just have to try, even when you're scared." Mari took a deep breath. Her dad was right—she had overcome challenges before. She looked at her dad and asked anxiously. "Where do we start?" Her dad chuckled and replied, "How about we start at the store?" "Race you to the car!" Mari shouted as she sprinted from the bench.

As Mari sat in the passenger seat on the way to the store, she started creating her supply list. She said to her dad, "Well, of course we'll need lots of ice, and even more flavors, cups, gloves, napkins, and spoons. " She looked at her dad and laughed, "I hope you brought your wallet". Mari's dad chuckled as they finally arrived at the store

Mari's mouth dropped at all of the flavors she could choose from. Bubblegum, Blue Raspberry, Mango, Pineapple, Lemon lime, Tiger's blood, Strawberry, Cherry, Banana, Grape, Fruit punch, Peach, and Watermelon. She asked, "What flavors should I get?" Her dad replied, "All of them!"

As they headed towards the register, Mari saw her friend Lisa. Both girls were excited to see each other. Lisa asked, "What are you doing with all these flavors?" Mari nervously replied, "I'm starting a snow cone business!" Lisa grinned, "OMG! That's so cool! I can't wait to try one!" "They'll be available soon!" Mari replied as she waved goodbye to Lisa.

Mari spent day and night practicing all the different flavors and perfecting her snow cones. But every time she thought about selling them, fear made her freeze. "I'm just a kid," she whispered to herself. "But tomorrow is the big day!"

That night, Mari laid in bed, staring at the ceiling, wondering how she could make her snow cone business even better. "What if I didn't just make snow cones for people, but also for their pets? Snow Dogs! They'd have shaved ice with whipped cream!" she thought excitedly as she rolled over and went to sleep.

The next day, Mari and her dad loaded the car, headed to the park, and set up her snow cone stand. "Another hot day," She thought to herself "This should be great for business." It was orange and blue, just as she had imagined. Taking a deep breath, she said, "I got this."

It didn't take long before a large crowd gathered ready to order snow cones. Mari whispered a quick prayer of thanks and got straight to work By the end of the day, everyone was satisfied and she was sold out. Wiping her forehead, she shouted, "I did it!" She had conquered her fear.

Mari realized something important: sometimes the scariest part is just beginning. But once you start, the possibilities are endless. Now, when Mari looks at her snow cone stand, she doesn't see fear—she sees flavor, fun, and success. Mari continues to inspire kids everywhere to dream big and start their own businesses. What business would you start?

Made in the USA
Las Vegas, NV
11 November 2024

11580177R10017